Humphrey loves to go camping,
Exploring new and old places is super exciting.
To find the best spot to camp Humphrey used his trusty map
and went for a long hike deep into the woods.

During his hike, Humphrey met a beautiful blue butterfly.
His new friend was so nice that he sat on Humphrey's nose.
Though the butterfly's feet did tickle.

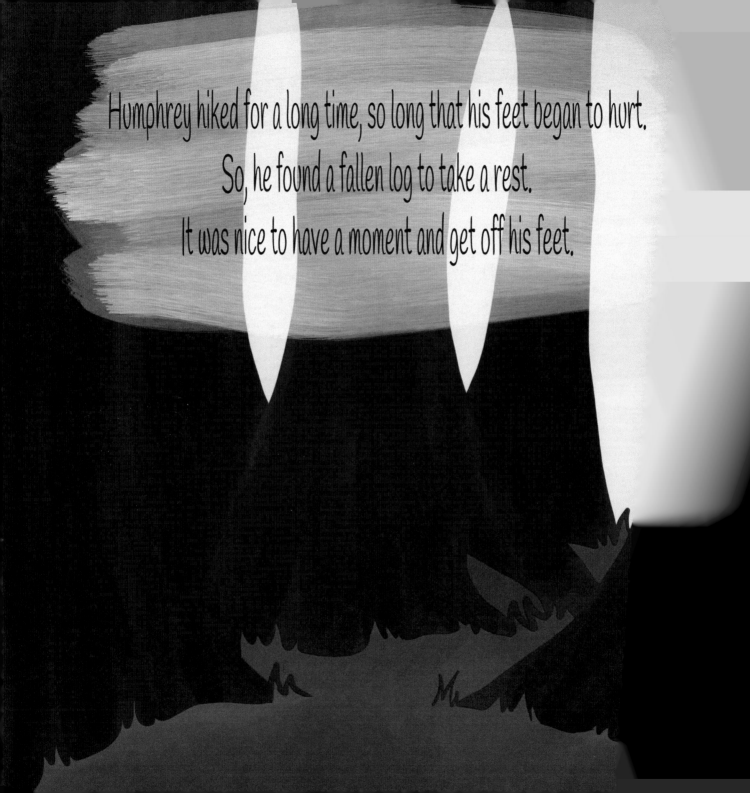

Humphrey hiked for a long time, so long that his feet began to hurt.
So, he found a fallen log to take a rest.
It was nice to have a moment and get off his feet.

Continuing on Humphrey finally found the perfect spot!
It was flat and clear of rocks so that it would be comfortable to sleep on
And now all he had to do was set up his tent.

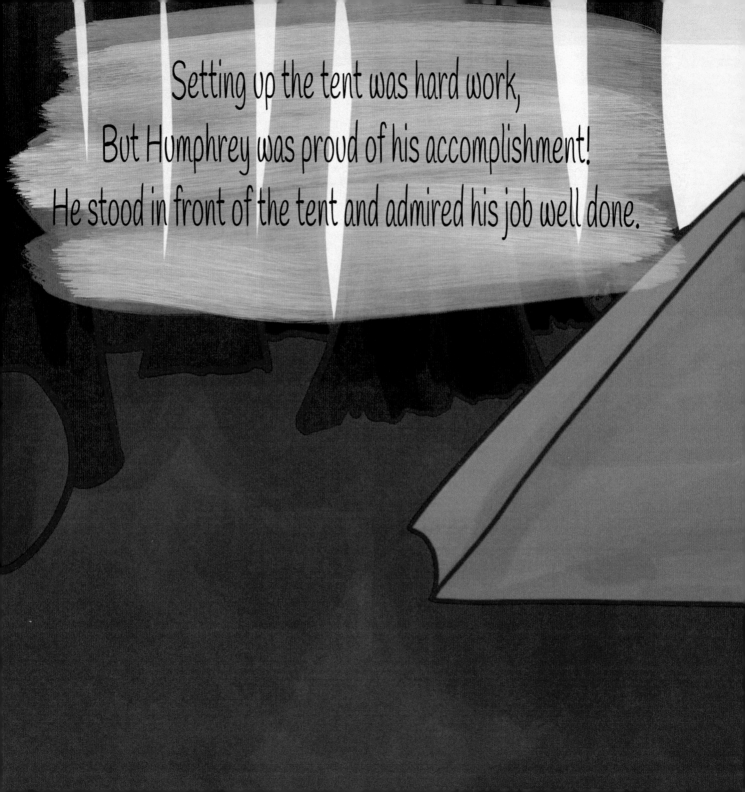

Setting up the tent was hard work,
But Humphrey was proud of his accomplishment!
He stood in front of the tent and admired his job well done.

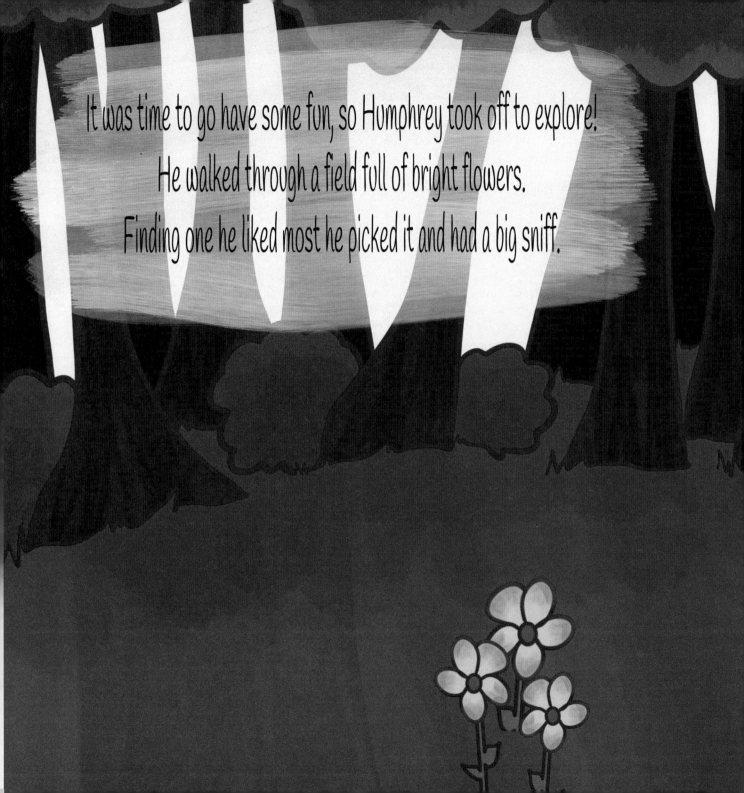

It was time to go have some fun, so Humphrey took off to explore!
He walked through a field full of bright flowers.
Finding one he liked most he picked it and had a big sniff.

Continuing his exploring he came across a new friend.

A little bird who sang a beautiful song.

He stayed and listened, giving the little bird the flower in return.

Next Humphrey found some mushrooms growing beside a tree.
Humphrey took out his handy plant book and laid down.
He inspected the mushrooms with excitement to learn what they were.

As Humphrey continued his trek, he looked up at the bright sun. It was getting low which means it would be dark before long. But Humphrey had one more activity that he wanted to do.

Humphrey grabbed his inner tube, aired it up, and went floating down the river. The water was nice and cool on the warm summer day, and it was moving at a steady pace. As the water took Humphrey for a ride, Humphrey noticed his friend Bear walking along.

Bear helped him out of the water so they could visit.
They sat together as Bear fished and this was something Bear was really good at.
Even though Humphrey did not eat fish, he still enjoyed sitting with his friend.

They talked for a long time,
So long that by the time Humphrey got back to camp it was dark outside.
So, Humphrey sat and roasted marshmallows over the campfire.

Humphrey had a full belly after eating a bunch of marshmallows.

Tired, he laid down beside the warm fire and looked up at the night sky.

As the night grew darker the moon became brighter.

He laid and admired the stars,
there were so many of them up there that it made him feel quite small.
But every star is different just like how every creature is unique.
And that thought made him feel incredibly special.

He laid under the stars until he began to grow sleepy.
It was too cold to sleep outside, so Humphrey put out his fire.
Then he crawled into his tent and bundled up.
Humphrey had a fun day, full of adventure and friends.
Humphrey loves to go camping.